ISBN 0-590-46285-7

Text copyright © 1985 by Richard Buckley.
Illustrations copyright © 1985 by Eric Carle.
All rights reserved. Published by Scholastic Inc.,
730 Broadway, New York, NY 10003, by arrangement with
Picture Book Studio.

12 11 10 9 8 7 6 5 4 3 2 1   3 4 5 6 7 8/9

Printed in the U.S.A.   08

First Scholastic printing, January 1993

The Foolish Tortoise

The Foolish Tortoise

SCHOLASTIC INC.

New York   Toronto   London   Auckland   Sydney

A tortoise, tired of being slow,
Impatient to get up and go,

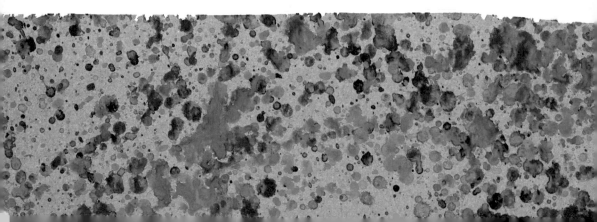

Took off his large and heavy shell
And left it lying where it fell.

"Hooray!" he cried, "Now I've been freed —
I'll see the world at double speed!"

Though faster, he was not express
And his protection was far less,
So when he heard a hornet's drone
The tortoise crept beneath a stone.

A hungry bird came swooping past.
He looked so fierce and flew so fast,
The tortoise hid behind some trees
And felt quite weak behind the knees.

"I don't feel safe, there's too much risk.
If only I could be more brisk!"
He headed for the riverbed:
A fish swam up, the tortoise fled.

Along his way our hero went
And almost had an accident.
A snake with open jaws slid near.
The tortoise backed away in fear.

A hare, a hound, a horse raced by —
So rapidly, they seemed to fly.
The tortoise gasped, sat goggle-eyed —
"I'll never be that quick," he sighed.

He wandered on, the sun rose high.
"I wish I had more shade!" he cried.
A sudden thunderstorm swept in,
And soaked the tortoise to the skin.

The wind rose up, and soon the breeze
Was bending branches in the trees.

The tortoise shivered, "Now I'm cold.
I wish I hadn't been so bold."

"I think I've lost the urge to roam
I think it's time that I went home."
"Without my shell I don't feel right."
So when his shell came into sight,

He climbed back in and said,
"Goodnight!"

Born in Syracuse, N.Y. in 1929, ERIC CARLE moved to Germany in 1935 with his parents. His schooling there included work under Ernst Schneidler at the Academy of Graphic Arts. He returned to America in 1952 and worked as a graphic designer for the New York Times, and later as art director for an international advertising agency. His first two books, 1,2,3 TO THE ZOO (1968), and THE VERY HUNGRY CATERPILLAR (1969), gained him immediate international recognition. The latter title, now considered a modern classic, has sold over 4 million copies and been translated into 14 languages.

He writes of his work: "When I first began to think about children's books, it reawakened in me struggles of my own childhood, touching an unfinished area of my own growing up. A child spends five years basically at home — a place of warmth, play and protection. Then school begins, and all of a sudden it is a world of schedule, abstraction, and organized learning. Very simply put, I decided I wanted to create books that make this transition easier."